Weekly Reader Children's Book Club presents

JOEY
AND THE
BIRTHDAY PRESENT

WEEKLY READER
CHILDREN'S BOOK CLUB ®

This is a registered trademark

Maxine Kumin
Anne Sexton

JOEY
AND THE
BIRTHDAY PRESENT
ILLUSTRATED BY EVALINE NESS

McGRAW-HILL BOOK COMPANY

New York · St. Louis · San Francisco · Dusseldorf
London · Mexico · Panama · Sydney · Toronto

Weekly Reader Children's Book Club Edition

For Joy, and the mouse she loved

Joey had never seen a cat. But all his life in the empty farmhouse he had heard stories about their sneaky ways. It was a cat that had eaten Joey's own grandfather right here on Buttonwood Farm.

Joey thought a cat might be as big as the stove and have whiskers as long as broomstraws. He thought its teeth might be as big as the coffee cups he and the other mice played hide-and-seek in. He thought its tail might be as thick as the trunk of the old apple tree in the pasture.

One summer day while Joey was humming to himself and shelling seed pods on the window ledge, he heard a strange sound. Something was coming up the driveway. Something on wheels. He knew from pictures he had seen in old magazines that this was a car. A car with people in it.

"Help! Help!" cried Joey. "The Buttonwoods are coming back!"

All the other mice sped to their secret passageways and were out of sight when the people came to the door. But Joey was so busy sounding the alarm that he forgot to hide. Besides, he was too curious to run away. The best he could do was to curl himself around the window lock and pretend not to be there. Even though he was terribly scared, Joey kept one eye open to spy on the new people. He saw a man, a woman, a little boy, and most especially he saw a terrible cat.

"Woof! woof!" said the cat.

Joey watched from a crack in the bookshelf as the man carried in two big suitcases. The woman followed, carrying a frying pan and a teakettle. Next came the little boy. He was carrying a cage with a strange white mouse inside it. *Why have they painted the mouse white?* Joey wondered. *I know! They are keeping it in the cage to feed to the cat some time soon.*

Joey ran back to the other mice in hiding.

"Listen, everybody!" he whispered. "I have seen the giant cat! He is white with black spots and his terrible toenails click when he walks. His tail is as thick as a chair leg and it thumps from side to side ten times a minute. And the noise this giant cat makes when he speaks is as large as a thunderstorm."

But no one agreed with Joey. Everyone's father said that the Buttonwood cat had been striped like a tiger. His toenails had never clicked when he walked, and if he swished his tail at all, he had swished it silently.

"Then this must be *new* people with a *new* cat," Joey said.

And everyone agreed.

Late that night, Joey was quietly pacing between the upstairs floorboards. He could think of nothing but the cat and the painted mouse. He could think of nothing but how it would feel to be eaten. He heard a small musical sound coming from the little boy's bedroom. It was not a mouse sound. It was a metal sound, as if someone were clicking two spoons together softly.

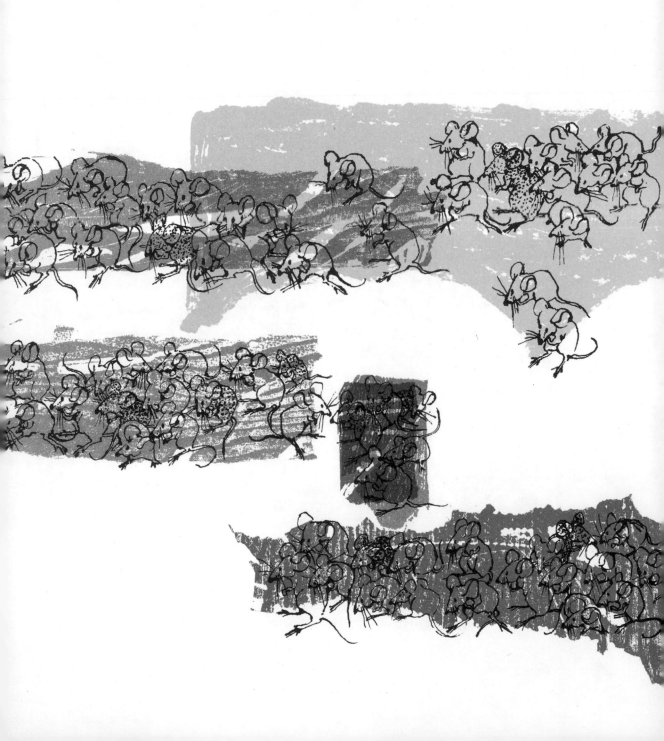

Carefully Joey crept into the bedroom. The little boy was asleep. On a table in the corner sat the mouse cage. The white mouse was running around and around a little wheel inside the cage, as though he were running away from an invisible cat. He was running so fast that he didn't even hear Joey jump up alongside.

"You poor thing," Joey said. "Are you in trouble? What are you running away from?"

"In the first place, I'm not a thing," said the white mouse. "My name is Prince. In the second place, you startled me terribly by jumping up here like that. Who are you, anyway?"

"My name is Joey. I *live* here. When are they going to feed you to that terrible cat?"

"Nonsense! There isn't any cat. And I live here, too. Inside this cage."

"One of us is crazy," Joey said, shaking his head. "I saw an enormous white cat downstairs with black spots and a thick tail. I even saw his big red mouth! He has sharp teeth and a red tongue that hangs out when he breathes."

Prince laughed and got down from his wheel. "That's only the dog. He's an old grandfather by now. He's no more dangerous than a sunflower seed. Why, whenever I am taken out of my cage, he lies down on the floor and puts his paws over his eyes."

"A dog? I can't believe it! So that's what a dog looks like! Wait 'till I tell the others!"

"You mean there are more than one of you?"

"Oh yes," Joey said cheerfully. "One hundred and four of us in all. Would you like to come and meet them?"

"Some other time, perhaps. I must get back to my exercise." Prince climbed back on his wheel.

"But what are you doing that for?"

"Merely to keep in shape."

"You mean you have to run in the same place all the time to keep in shape? That sounds pretty dull to me. We run in the field and all over the place— between the floors and up and down stairs, if we feel like it."

"How common! You get so dirty that way. Just look at your fur, for instance. You've gotten yourself all brown and gray from something."

"What do you mean, all brown and gray? That's my natural color. I'm a field mouse, you know. Anyway, look at you! Why did you let them paint you all white?"

"Nonsense," said Prince. "That isn't paint. It's my natural color. I'm a purebred white mouse from Finnorty's Pet Shop."

"Is that where you got those pink eyes, too?" Joey asked. "In the pet shop?"

"Sure," said Prince. "Right between the parakeets and the goldfish." Then he asked Joey, "Is that where you got those brown eyes, too? In the field?"

"Sure," Joey answered. "Right between the rhubarb and the cabbage."

They both laughed.

"Want to try out my wheel?" Prince asked.

"Okay." Joey wedged the door open with a crayon and jumped on the wheel with his new friend. After they had run around for a minute in each direction, Joey said, "Want to come see all our hiding places?"

"Well," Prince said doubtfully. "Is it safe out there?"

"If you're with me, you'll be safe," Joey promised.

First they visited Joey's cousins who lived in five
nests, each the size of an apple, in an old mattress.

Next they called on his aunts and uncles in the medicine chest and finally they dropped in on all the grandparents who lived in a downstairs cupboard drawer.

Joey's immediate family had settled for years in nests they had made in the top burners of the gas stove. But now it was Moving Day. Prince and Joey helped to carry their bedding up to a secret corner of the attic.

Later that night, Prince proudly showed Joey around his cage.

"This is my bed," he said, pointing to a little heap of cotton batten in one corner. "It is changed twice a week. Here is my mirror to see myself in. It's really there so I won't get lonely."

Joey peered in beside him. "So that's what we look like!" The two mice spent a long time making faces and sticking out their tongues in the mirror.

"Here is my personal water supply," Prince said. He showed Joey the small bottle with its special spout and Joey sucked on it.

"The little boy takes good care of me," Prince said. "He cups me in his hand and he carries me around in his pocket when we travel. His mother doesn't like me much, so I have to be careful not to squeak when we go outside together."

"Don't you get seasick riding around in a pocket all the time?" Joey asked.

"Not at all," said Prince. "You ought to come along next time and see what it's like."

"Not *me*," said Joey. "I'm afraid of people."

"I don't care for them too much myself," Prince admitted. "But the little boy is special. He is my friend. And look what good food he gives me. This is tonight's dinner." They both tasted some oatmeal mixed with peanut butter. Joey found it a bit sticky, but delicious.

The next night, Prince came running in the field with Joey. There he ate his first dried raspberry and his first mosquito. He found the mosquito a bit salty, but delicious.

Each night Joey taught Prince something new. Together they went exploring between the walls of the house and came out coated with plaster dust. They ran through the attic, trailing little bits of insulation. Up from the cellar they scampered, leaving small damp footprints behind them. They skated around and around on a forgotten can of bacon fat. They feasted on an open box of crackers and scattered the crumbs all along the counter.

By the middle of the summer, Prince knew that the little boy was watching them. Although he lay very still and never spoke, his eyes were open almost every night.

"He wants to be your friend, too," Prince told Joey. "Come on. Let's keep him company. I know a warm, safe hiding place."

Joey shook with fear, but he followed Prince into the little boy's pajama pocket. They curled up together. It was dark inside and smelled of soap.

"What's that terrible noise?" Joey asked. "And why are we bobbing up and down?"

Prince laughed. "What you hear is the little boy's heart beating. And we are moving up and down because he is breathing. Do you like it?"

"It's sort of fun," Joey agreed.

The little boy giggled and the two mice bobbed up and down even faster. From then on they visited his pocket regularly.

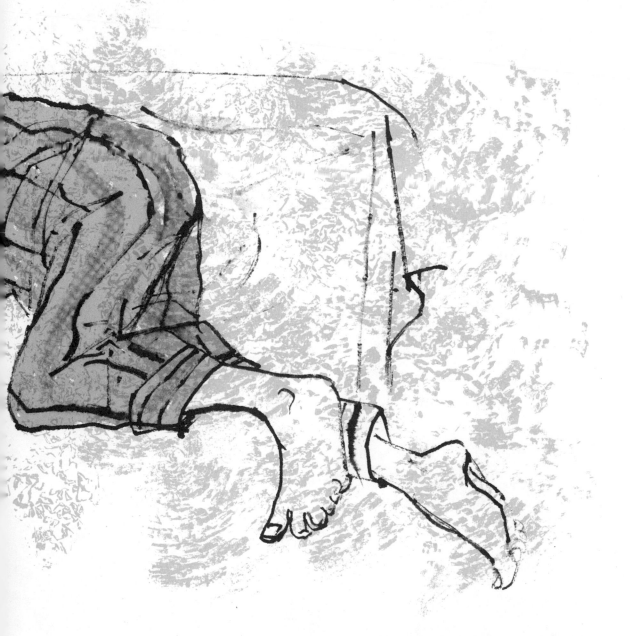

"I like your little boy," Joey told Prince. "The only trouble is, we mice have to hide from his mother and father. It is hard to be quiet all the time. But we have a plan. We are going to move out of the farmhouse and go camping in the field beside the pond."

Prince's pink eyes got bigger and bigger. "You mean you're going to live out there in the open with wolves and owls and all? That's too scary."

Joey laughed. "We'll be safe as long as it's summer. We're digging nine burrows with exits and entrances. But I don't know what we'll do when winter comes."

"Move back into the farmhouse, of course," said Prince. "We all go back to the city in September. We only come here in the summer."

"You mean you can't live here always?" Joey asked. "Who will let you out of the cage in the night?"

"No one," Prince said sadly. "I'll be all alone. But I won't think about that now."

The rest of the summer, the two mice spent every night together. Some nights they woke the old dog in the living room and danced in front of him until he put his paws over his eyes. Some nights they played hide-and-seek in the coffee cups, and once they even got into the popcorn. Some nights they visited the campers in their field by the pond and listened to the bullfrogs. And some nights they just sat in Prince's cage and talked about life.

"Tell me again about the monkey in the pet shop," Joey would say. And Prince told.

"Tell me again about the terrible cat who ate your grandfather," Prince would say. And Joey told.

Suddenly, all too soon, it was September. The swamp maples were turning red. Most of the mosquitoes were gone. Prince grew sadder and sadder. He knew that in a few more days he would lose his summer friend.

"I know something that will cheer you up," Joey said one night. And he raced Prince down to the kitchen table where someone had forgotten to put the lid on the blackberry jam.

They ate so much that their stomachs bulged. Their whiskers and paws were all sticky and purple.

"I'm stuffed!" Joey said. "Isn't this jam a pretty color? Let's go finger paint on the piano keys."

But they did not only make blackberry paintings. Some rather funny music came forth at midnight in the quiet old farmhouse.

Suddenly the little boy's mother loomed over them with a dust pan and brush.

"Look out, Prince!" Joey shouted. "Run for your life! Run for the hole in the baseboard!"

But Prince's sticky feet and city ways slowed him down. From his hiding place, Joey watched helplessly as the woman brushed his friend into the dustpan and carried him off.

The next night when Joey came at his usual hour, the cage was wired shut with a large black hairpin. The little boy lay silently in his bed, pretending to be asleep. As Joey watched, a large tear rolled down his cheek.

"He's crying because his mother thought he let me out of my cage last night," Prince explained. "And he's sad because now I can't play with you any more."

"I bet I can undo that hairpin," Joey said. "There's a nail in the tool box down cellar that would pry it loose."

"Better not try," said Prince. "I don't want the little boy to get into any more trouble."

Now they could only sit with the bars between them and talk.

On their last night together, Joey brought Prince two cake crumbs as a going-away present. But as they crouched and nibbled together, the little boy quietly got out of bed. He undid the hairpin and propped the cage door open with a crayon. Then he jumped back in bed and shut his eyes tightly as if nothing at all had happened.

Prince whispered to Joey. "See what the little boy has done? He knows this is our last time together. He knows we are leaving for the city tomorrow. And he is giving me a chance to run away with you."

"Oh, please!" Joey said. "Now you can stay. You can stay here with me on Buttonwood Farm."

"If only I could," Prince said.

"But you can. It's easy. Even the little boy thinks

so. We will live in the left front burner of the stove all winter."

"Easy for you, Joey. But I am a tame white mouse from Finnerty's Pet Shop. I cannot live on seed pods and berries. I belong in a cage."

"Oh, Prince. Don't say that. You could learn."

"Maybe I could," Prince said sadly, "but the little boy needs me. I am his only pet."

"He has the dog," Joey said. "Besides, he wants you to go."

"No. The dog belongs to the parents. They got him a long time ago, before the little boy was born. He needs me. You see, I am his birthday present."

And they both agreed that a birthday present could not run away.

In the city, Prince's cage sits in front of a window looking over the snowy rooftops. The room is warm and the oatmeal and peanut butter are tasty. Some nights Prince climbs into the little boy's pajama pocket and bobs up and down all by himself. But he often thinks of Joey and the one hundred and three other mice on Buttonwood Farm. He wishes summer would hurry. Prince is all alone. He exercises every night on his wheel. Then he spends a lot of time looking into the mirror.

The Authors

In addition to their respective national reputations on the poetry scene, Maxine Kumin and Anne Sexton are close friends who enjoy collaborating on books for young people. Readers will remember their entertaining EGGS OF THINGS.

Maxine Kumin lives with her family in Newton, Massachusetts. She has written more than a dozen children's books, including the popular BEACH BEFORE BREAKFAST. She is also the author of two adult novels and three poetry collections.

Anne Sexton makes her home in Weston, Massachusetts, with her husband and two children. The author of four poetry collections, she has received many honors for her work, including the Pulitzer Prize for Poetry, awarded in 1967.

The Artist

A distinguished author in her own right, Evaline Ness has illustrated many outstanding books for young people. Miss Ness grew up in Pontiac, Michigan, and attended art schools in Chicago, Washington, D.C., New York, and Italy.

The recipient of the Caldecott medal for SAM, BANGS & MOONSHINE, Miss Ness also has three Caldecott runners-up to her credit: TOM TIT TOT, A POCKETFUL OF CRICKET, and ALL IN THE MORNING EARLY.